KILLER SANTA

A Christmas Horror Story

Todd Condit

ISBN-13: 9798712359493
ISBN-10: 1477123456

Cover design by: David Washburn
Library of Congress Control Number: 2018675309
Printed in the United States of America

CONTENTS

KILLER SANTA

A Christmas Horror Story

By Todd Condit

CHAPTER 1: JORDAN

It's a big day for Jordan. It was only two days till his favorite holiday and the first time in his miserable life that he gathered up the necessary courage to try out for his dream. To be Santa Claus would be amazing and to play him at the local Christmas festival, even better.

A fresh dusting of snow falls outside the section 8 housing where Jordan is currently sleeping. His bed, an old box spring twin that he found at a yard sale a few years back, rests directly on the floor in the corner of his one-room shit hole.

Jordan lies under a dirty sheet, just a blanket-covered lump softly snoring away in the morning. The only illumination is a string of classic over-sized Christmas lights, the ones that explode quickly when you throw them on the ground, carelessly draped across the kitchen countertop and hung by push pins around the perimeter of the walls.

A beat-up brown recliner sits in front of a re-frigerator box that is currently being used as a coffee table. It's littered with old boxes of pizza and various fast food cartons. Two-liter soda bottles filled with different shades of dark yellow liquid are strewn about. One of which slowly drips onto the floor through a cap that was not closed correctly.

An old wooden boxed TV, straight out of 1995, sits front and center in the room. Rabbit ears pro-trude at bent angles, apparently set in a way to pick up whatever local programming was available to him.

Most guys his age that are lacking a significant

other are either into video games, movies, or some kind of epic role-playing game.

But Jordan is different. There are no posters of the newest superhero or a bikini-clad movie star. Instead, his room is covered with Santa Claus and Christmas decorations.

Sloppily cut magazine pictures are tacked up in various places around the studio, featuring cartoon caricatures of a happy Santa handing out toys, to full-on holiday cake displays. A half-lit, almost dying plastic blow mold of a jolly St. Nick with a couple of reindeer eating out of his palm sits on the countertop. And the cream of the crop, last year's dumpster discovery. A brand new (to Jordan) five-foot Christmas tree with the fake snow glued onto it, the kind that falls off with the slightest touch and ends up everywhere. He couldn't believe his luck when he found it outside the Twin Pines Mall last year, complete with various ornaments and built-in lighting.

The sudden alarm from his cracked smartphone pulls Jordan from his slumber. As he dismisses the alarm, he notices a calendar alert through the broken display.

"Santa Tryouts 10:30 AM" It produces an instant smile on Jordan's face.

Usually, a broad smile brought on by the sheer joy of a Santa tryout would make anyone's heart melt. Unfortunately, nobody would ever describe this smile as "warm." Dental hygiene has never been a worry for Jordan; swishing his mouth with day-old soda is good enough for him. The teeth that he does have are all in some form of decay. And the breath, let's just say it's a blessing nobody ever gets close enough to him to smell it.

Excited for the day to begin, he springs from his bed. He isn't exactly the type you would associate with playing Santa Claus. His tighty whities, the smallest adult brand one can buy, hang off him like loose skin. His holey white shirt is in similar disrepair with plenty of pizza and unknown source stains.

He was born with one leg slightly shorter than the other, which causes him to have a subtle limp. His disability does nothing but highlights his tall, slim, almost severely malnourished body. Standing at 6 foot 3 inches and weighing in at 140 pounds on a good day, Jordan isn't exactly the text-book definition of "in shape."

All his life, he's had to deal with side-eyed looks or people crossing the street to avoid walking near him. Rude comments about him are something he's tried to block out, but he hears them regardless, echoing around his mind throughout the day.

He limps to his kitchen table, another yard sale find, and picks up a worn-out red flyer. "Santa tryouts, When: 12/23/2020 10:30 AM, Where: Our Church of the Savior, must have your own costume," says Jordan as he reads the flyer outline for the 100th time. He carefully folds the flyer with a loving touch as if it were a priceless heirloom and places it in the strap of his underwear.

Not much of an eater unless it's fast food and greasy, Jordan heads to his coat closet and selects the only item that seems to be well taken care of out of his belongings. A pristine red and white Santa suit. Complete with hat, beard, and belt. The only thing missing is a polished pair of black boots. But his worn and faded black Converse All-Stars will suffice. He just hopes the judges at the church don't hold it against him.

Jordan walks with a purpose to the kitchen and grabs a medicine bottle filled with big white pills. He shakes two into his palm, pops them into his mouth, and lets the sink faucet fill his open palm before using it to swallow them down. "Take two pills every four hours" stares back at him from the medicine label as he sets it back down on the counter with a look of distaste.

He walks to a propped bike in the corner with a green bicycle helmet perched atop the seat, and pauses as he catches himself in the mirror; what peers back at him would be alarming to others, but not to Jordan.

He doesn't see the darkness in his eyes. He does not know how the cheap, ill-fitting costume, almost two sizes too big, just makes his tall and slim figure look scary. He sees what he wants to see, what he hopes others will see. He sees Santa.

"You got this; this is yours. Make them see," he mutters to himself. Satisfied with the way he looks,

Jordan straps his helmet to his greasy head and grabs his bike. He is ready to start the day, and secure what is rightfully his. Santa.

CHAPTER 2: PETER

Peter is a friendly enough person. Easy going with an air about him that just bleeds "cool." Not like "*The Fonz*" cool but just easy-going and laid back, someone that everyone seems to like without much effort.

So getting a job at the local church to help out with the Christmas festival was right up his alley. He wouldn't say he was an ultra-religious person, but being around the churchgoers was usually a good time. Plus, the girls, "you know what they say about church girls," is a frequent line he would feed his buddies as he talked about his latest conquest.

In his mid-twenties, Peter wasn't sure what he wanted to end up doing for the rest of his life. Figuring out the future wasn't a priority; right now, he was content with just existing.

Peter nods to Tony, the church director, as he walks towards the main office. To call this a church would be an understatement. Not as big as one of those super churches you see on TV that scam millions in tax-free money from the sheep, but not far from it.

At this point, it was more of a corporation than a place of worship. The grounds themselves are very business-like. If you didn't see the 50-foot cross out front, you would assume it was an office building. The grounds are situated near the main road with a large parking lot, which doubled as the festival grounds and butted up to a stream that was always full of water.

But Peter didn't care about all that. He was

just happy to have a seasonal job, even if it was being the church bitch. For every game tent Peter helped to set up, a pile of fresh kid vomit was waiting for a good mopping. It paid the bills and paid for the steady stream of dates, and that's all he needed right now.

"Peter, how are you today?" says Tony with a look of boredom on his face.

"Not bad, Tony, just setting up some of the festival games like Tommy asked," says Peter.

Tommy is Tony's second in command. Small in stature, Tommy is the very definition of having "little man's syndrome."Always quick to look down at you and throw you under the bus with Tony.

Tony begins to walk towards the church, passing by various game tents, food tables, and Christmas displays for the festival. Peter, taking the hint, walks after him.

"Very good, very good. As you know, Peter, we're having the Santa tryouts today. Keep an eye out for any candidates that show up, and make sure they make it to the party hall. Can you handle that?"

"Yes sir, of course," replies Peter, thinking to himself how much of a prick Tony is. *But hey, he signs my checks.* Tony was a pompous asshole with way too much confidence for someone built like Homer Simpson. But as long as your work gets done, he mostly leaves you alone.

Tony, feeling smug that Peter referred to him as "sir," does his best impersonation of a genuine human smile and walks away. Tony is a man that demands respect. In his eyes, always being the smartest man in the room means that he will demand nothing short of perfection in all aspects of his business.

Being the Director of a mid-level church meant that Tony had control over every idiot that walked through the door on Sunday mornings. Tony, not religious in the slightest, chuckles to himself as he walks to the door.

———

A few hours later, while Peter is busy setting up the "Funnel Cake" tent, a strange sight pedals through the parking lot and into the main festival grounds area. A skinny man in his mid 30's wearing an ill-fitting Santa costume rolls to a stop a few feet from Peter and leans his tiny bike against the almost complete tent.

Frantic and sweaty, he says, "Is this where the Santa tryouts are?" Peter, being the polite person that he is, answers with his usual friendly demeanor. "More or less. This is where the Christmas festival will take place; the tryouts are in the party hall with Tony," says Peter, gesturing over his shoulder towards the main entrance.

Jordan follows his gesture and a look of unshakable determination settles over him. He takes off his bicycle helmet, half-heartedly smoothing his greasy, unkempt long black hair before pulling his wadded-up Santa hat from his pocket and placing it on his head as if it were a king's crown.

Peter can't help but think that this is the weirdest fucking thing he's seen in a while. "Uh, you can leave your bike and helmet against the table if you want. I'll walk you over to the hall and get you squared away." Peter says.

As Peter is speaking, Jordan's determined gaze slowly fades into a distant empty look. To Peter, it looks like he simply zoned out. Jordan feels himself slipping but is powerless to stop it.

He sees this man, standing in a half-made Christmas festival set up, but is in his own world now. When he gets like this, Jordan feels like everyone and everything is just a shadow. That he's passing through time observing but not actually being.

Once, he had visited a clinic and told them about these episodes. The doctor said something about being disconnected from reality. The medicine they gave him was supposed to eliminate the trances, drown out the voice that would sometimes whisper to him from the darkest recesses of his mind. And for the most part, they worked, except when he was stressed, the pills helped drown out most of his evil thoughts.

"You need to show them," the voice whispers in Jordan's mind.

Jordan hears Peter asking if he's ok and snaps out of it. "Yes, fine, please take me to the tryout. This is my day, you know. Finally, you will all see me," says Jordan.

Peter, puzzled, simply nods and begins walking towards the church. Jordan follows a few steps behind taking in the festival in its current state. The after-effects of his disconnection slip away and are replaced with a sense of wonder and hope. *This is it*, he thinks. *I'm going to be Santa this year.*

CHAPTER 3: THE BEAR

Peter leads Jordan through a typical office. Not what you would imagine a church office to look like. There was no personality, no religious decorations, nothing comforting, but that doesn't register with Jordan. Tailing behind Peter with his slight limp, Jordan marvels at the various boxes of Christmas decorations, fair-style food supplies, prizes for carnival-like games, and many seasonal items.

Something catches Jordan's eye, and he quickly shuffles over to a box filled to the brim with teddy bears of all colors. He picks up a white bear dressed in a little Santa costume and inspects it as a child would.

Peter notices Jordan has stopped and walks over to him. "Hey....." he realizes he doesn't know his name, "I never caught your name." Says Peter.

"Jordan," he says, never taking his eyes from the bear. Peter observes him as he awkwardly stares at the bear. "You know," says Peter, "You can have that if you want, we have like a million of them in storage." Jordan's eyes open in surprise.

"Are you serious?" Jordan asks with a voice full of wonder.

"Hell yeah dude, take a few. And call me Peter. Just stick them in your pocket so the boss doesn't see it," says Peter. "Come on, let's get you to the audition." Jordan grabs another two bears and stuffs them into his pockets. He keeps the first bear out as a sort of good luck totem and turns to follow Peter.

———————

They turn down a long, brightly lit hallway with a set of double doors at the end. A similar-looking Santa Tryouts flyer that Jordan had lovingly stuck in his underwear strap is taped to the door. Peter gives him a smile and slaps Jordan lightly on the back.

Peter says, "Good luck dude, I'll keep your bike safe while you're gone." Jordan gives Peter a nervous nod and shoves the bear into his waistband, pulling his Santa coat down to make sure the bear doesn't poke out.

He walks towards the double doors, mumbling to himself along the way. Peter looks at him for a while before shrugging his shoulders and going back to the Funnel Cake tent.

Jordan mumbles, "This is your time, and this is your destiny. Nobody is going to stop me. Nobody is going to hold me back. I'll make them all see." He begins to slip into one of his trances when he hears a distinct shout of "NEXT!" coming from the double doors.

The doors open and a portly fellow in his 50's exits. He's chubby, has a self-grown full white beard, but he's not Santa. Jordan is. By the look on his solemn face, it appears that the church judges don't see him as Santa either, great news for Jordan.

The rejected Santa glances up in Jordan's direction as they pass one another. His solemn look turns to one of disgust as he takes Jordan's frightening appearance in. But Jordan doesn't mind; he's used to the looks. Jordan's rancid smell hits the man's nostrils which causes him to grimace in disgust.

Jordan pauses at the doors and makes some last-minute adjustments to his costume. Fluffs the beard, straightens the cap. Good to go. He takes a deep breath and exhales slowly. Having composed himself, he reaches out and raps his knuckles against the door.

CHAPTER 4: THE AUDITION

The room is too big for an audition, more like a room for a large gathering. But Tony, or as he insists on being called while working, Mr. Franks, prefers it this way. The big room makes the people trying out nervous and off-balance. Making it that much easier for him to fuck with them.

The room is full of windows casting the late morning sun through them, illuminating the long table with a chair on either end—one for Tony, the other for his future Santa. Tommy, Tony's right-hand man, stands behind him like a fat little shadow.

Tommy learned long ago that when official business is taking place, he needs to be ready to spring to action at Tony's every beck and call. He's the assistant director after all, and he takes his role seriously.

Tony holds out his hand over his shoulder without looking. Tommy, always on point, grabs a bottle of water, loosens the cap, and places it in Tony's waiting hand, who takes it without thanking him.

"I tell you fucking what Tommy. These bastards get worse each year we have this damn event. I have half a mind to shut the whole damn festival down. Fuck em, not like these ungrateful pukes deserve it. I mean, have you seen the piss poor turnout of the collection plates lately? You'd swear we were running a cocksucking charity. This is a church for God's sake!"

He takes a long gulp from his water bottle.

During the rant, Tommy nods and grins in agreement. Tommy is too old to be a *yes-man ass kisser*, but he's always looked for someone to latch onto. His entire life has had him hanging onto someone else's coattails. Being very weak-willed was a perfect choice to be Tony's lackey. Short and soft yet full of himself due to his limited authority, Tommy is the textbook definition of a little bitch.

Tommy says, "You ain't wrong, Tony." Tony turns slightly in his chair, an annoyed look plastered across his middle-aged, neatly trimmed, bearded face.

"What the fuck is with this Tony shit?!" Tony exclaims, annoyed at the sudden disrespect Tommy has displayed. He mashes a pointed finger repeatedly into the table.

"When we are in the church, you refer to me as Mr. Franks. This isn't the fucking schoolyard Tommy for Christ's sake."

Tony leans back in his chair and takes another gulp from the now half-full water bottle. He thinks to himself how fucking dumb Tommy is. Dumb but loyal to a fault. Tony knows he's great at manipulating people to get what he wants, but fuck, Tommy is as easy as they get. Tommy would probably suck his dick if it meant getting a raise. He chuckles to himself as Tommy heads to the door and opens it.

Tommy opens the door and turns to a sight that he didn't expect to see today, or *ever* for that matter. Sure, hopeful Santa's would be in and out today, but this... this was just plain fucked up. He didn't even try to hide the "bottom to top" motion he usually reserved for some of the better-looking church girls.

Faded and worn black Converse All-Stars. At least two sizes too big, cheap red Santa pants. A vinyl belt looped two times over this rail of a person's torso. Equally cheap Santa coat. But the face. God, the face. Pockmarked, greasy skin poked out beneath a cheap Santa beard. Complete with a rotted mouth smiling down at him. A cheap hat sits on top of a mat of long greasy black hair.

Jordan, looking at Tommy with his best smile, says, "Hi."

Tommy attempts to compose himself, but there is something off about this creep. He just has an aura of wrongness about him that seems to seep into the surrounding environment. Tommy clears his throat, "Umm, come on in and have a seat." He gestures towards the empty chair.

Jordan nervously shuffles and takes a seat at the far side of the table. Tommy looks at Tony with a shocked looked and mouths, "What the fuck?" Tony, slightly taken aback by this monstrosity of a Santa before him, composes himself as Tommy takes his ass kisser position behind him.

"And you are?" asks Tony with a hint of disgust in his voice.

"Jo...Jordan," says Jordan in a nervous stutter. He doesn't usually stutter, but considering the circumstances, he couldn't help it.

Jordan settles into the chair and nervously fiddles with the position of his hands. *Should I put them in my lap, on the table, dangle them to the sides?* He thinks before settling on placing them clasped together on the table in front of them.

The room is silent. Tommy barely hides the disgust on his face as he peers at Jordan, continuing to take him all in. Ever the asshole lackey, he leans in to whisper in Tony's ear. They glance at Jordan as whatever joke, clearly at Jordan's expense, makes them both chuckle. Tony, trying to remain professional, gestures for Tommy to return back to his place behind him and clears his throat before speaking.

"So, uh, Jackson... what..."

Tony is cut off mid-sentence by Jordan trying to correct his name. "It's Jordan, uh, sir." Tony doesn't miss a beat and continues his thought. "Right... Jordan. So, you're obviously here for the Santa tryouts judging by that.... outfit you're wearing."

"Yes sir, been practicing my lines as well, trying to get them perfect for the Christmas festival," replies Jordan in a confident tone.

"Great, just great. Listen, kid. I'm just going to come out and say it; you're just not the Santa type. We're looking for someone, well, less freaky. You do know kids will be present, right? Do you think our fine people will want their little ones sitting on *your* lap, whispering their Christmas requests into that mop you have on your head? I sure as hell do not," says Tony.

During this initial rant, Jordan does not falter. He's heard it all before, from when he was a kid getting picked on in elementary school up to now. Insults he can handle. Sideways looks? Not a problem.

Tommy starts to nod his head in agreement, a small smile forming on his lips. He reassures Tony's rants with an "mmhmm" sound, which gets Tony going even more.

Tony continues his verbal onslaught. "This isn't St. Marks down the street or that terrible church over in Elmdale run by that fucker Father Matt. This is Our Church of the Savior. This is the show, kid. And for you to even think of coming in here with that half-assed costume, shit, I don't even know what to think. Maybe an Elf but Santa, the big man? No. Fucking. Way."

Jordan begins to panic internally. *Every Time I want something, this happens. Some asshole gets in my way. They never change. All of them are the same.*

"I, uh, have a lot more to offer than an Elf. Listen. I can get a new costume. Or wait, listen to my ho ho I can do." Jordan lets out his best Santa impersonation, which instantly brings Tony and Tommy to laughter.

"Can you believe this fucking guy, Tony?" Tommy yells out as he laughs hysterically.

"Listen, guy. The short answer is this," says Tony.

Jordan leans forward in his seat, a flutter of

hope grows in his abdomen. He doesn't seem to notice that they are laughing at him after his *Ho Ho Ho* impersonation, not with him.

"No....Every. Fucking. Time. No," Tony states, leaning back in his chair while interlocking his fingers behind his head.

Jordan's eyes sink to his hands. He cannot believe this. He put so much effort into his costume. His fucking Santa voice. He feels himself going into one of his trances. But this time, he doesn't completely tune out what's being said.

"But the long answer.....no fucking way kid. You look like a fucking crack head Slenderman in a Santa costume," says Tony

Tommy and Tony are bouncing one liners off of one another at Jordan's expense, laughing hysterically along the way. All the while, Jordan slips deeper and deeper into his melancholy trance.

"Good one, sir! I know who to ask if we run out of cooking oil, look at that greasy fucking head!" shouts Tommy as he points and laughs at Jordan.

"This dude really thinks his skinny ass can pull off Santa? That suit can fit like three more of his creepy asses in it and still have room!" Tony slams his fist down, so very pleased with his epic joke. The room, according to Jordan, seems to dim. The voices, while heard, seem to fade into the distance.

His eyes gloss over, a thin line of drool falls out of his now tilting head. *"No more,"* the voice speaks in his head. The room slowly zooms into his face until it all at once snaps back into focus.

"These cocksuckers get worse and worse Tommy, I mean, every year we get bad candidates, but this creepy bastard takes the trophy," says Tony.

Tommy stops laughing and becomes fixated on Jordan. Tony, not knowing why Tommy is not laughing anymore, follows his gaze to what he's looking at. Slowly, Jordan adjusts his head and stares at the two men across from him. A wide grin slowly forms, giving way to a mouth filled with rot.

Tony gestures to Jordan, "Ok, we're done here, Tommy; get this freak out of here." Jordan hears the name "freak," and his smile widens. Tommy reluctantly walks over and gestures to Jordan to get up. Jordan follows Tommy with a slow turn of his smiling head as he gets nearer.

"Uh, time to go, Jay," says Tommy.

Jordan wipes the drool from his mouth with the back of his hand, the sudden movement startling Tommy. "It's Jordan," Jordan says, in a calm but surprisingly forceful manner. Jordan gets up slowly, pushes in his chair, and puts out his hand for Tommy to shake, a sheen of drying saliva visible on the hand. Tommy nervously snaps a look to Tony, who nods in encouragement.

Tommy reluctantly takes his hand and shakes it while Jordan stares down at him into his eyes. Tommy can't help but feel unnerved at the sight of this smiling crazy looking Santa. The feeling that he had when he opened the door comes back full force. A sense of dread, an overwhelming sense of wrongness, pours out of Jordan.

"Well...uh... no hard feelings, right? You're just not the right person," says Tommy. He stops shaking Jordan's hand and attempts to pull his back, but it is firmly in Jordan's boney, clammy grip.

"None at all. I'll be seeing you," says Jordan. He looks at Tony and gives a nod. He lets Tommy's hand go and then makes his way to the door but stops as he grabs the doorknob.

"Merry Christmas," says Jordan, peering over his shoulder, a slight smirk on his face. He opens and exits the door, leaving his hopes and the rest of his sanity behind.

When the door closes, both men let out a sigh of relief and look at each other. Tommy fishes a hand sanitizer out of his pocket and quickly cleans his hands, not knowing what the hell kind of germs could have been on that weirdo. Not to mention the sheen of drying saliva that his thumb firmly planted in when he shook his hand.

Tony leans back in his chair and covers his eyes. "Tommy, I'm just straight, not having a good time right now." Both men remained silent, reflecting on how weird that guy was. Sure they were harsh, but this was Tony's church, and nothing was going to ruin the festival and potentially tarnish his good name.

CHAPTER 5: THANKS FOR THE BEARS

Peter was outside working on a crowd favorite, the remote control train track. A favorite not only because all the kids seemed to love trains, but also because there was a small red enclosed bridge that spanned the stream's width.

A few years ago, before he worked here, they had to enclose the bridge since they were losing too many trains into the stream, which at this time of the year was either completely frozen, causing them to shatter on impact, or was overfilled with freezing rushing water which led to them disappearing into the swift current.

As he was finishing touching up the mini barn paint that sat at a corner of the track, he noticed Jordan exiting the main building. He got up and walked over to him. Jordan didn't seem to see Peter and kept his gaze to the ground. When he was within a few feet, Peter called out.

"How'd it go, Jordan?" asked Peter

Jordan stopped and looked up at Jordan with indifference. " Great," Jordan muttered.

"So you got the gig?" asked Peter as he dusted some dried paint flakes from his fingers.

"Nope! But it doesn't matter anymore. I know what I have, and I know what I am. And nobody, not you, not those two in there, is going to stop me. You'll see," said Jordan.

"Whoa man, I didn't say anything to you," Peter says defensively.

Jordan's eyes began to glaze over as he felt the beginnings of one of his trances. He rushed off towards his bike, which was propped against the funnel cake stand. "Whatever, thanks for the bears," said Jordan over his shoulder as he steps up to his bike.

Peter stares at him as he mounts the bike and awkwardly rides out of the festival grounds. *Tony and his butt buddy must have really put that guy through hell.* He had seen multiple candidates go into the audition happy but come out downtrodden. Jordan must have had a similar fate to all the other rejects. *Oh well, not my problem.* He turns and goes back to his duties.

———————

Jordan is having an internal struggle as he rides his bike in shame. His helmet, unstrapped and askew on his head, bounces on top of his Santa hat with each bump. "I'm done with these people. I'm done with everyone," he mutters to himself.

He thinks back to his childhood, getting pushed in the mud by Brandon Doyle after school for being, as he had put it, a faggot freak. His whore mom having a revolving door of deadbeats in and out of their rundown trailer. That cunt of a principal Miss Banks blaming him for "not trying hard enough to fit in" with the other kids. So what if he didn't like playing football with all the other meatheads? He wasn't a jock. So what if he didn't participate in the afterschool Dungeons and Dragons league? He wasn't a fucking nerd.

And now this. That bald fuck Tony saying all those things was one thing. That sniveling little twerp Tommy, smirking and giggling was another. But to be denied playing his dream role by that chubby piece of shit was the last straw. These mother fuckers will pay, all of them. I'm going to do whatever the fuck I want, and whoever tries to stop me will be sorry.

It was well past the 4-hour maximum window to take his mania medication. When Jordan got like this, it was hard to stop. Usually, he would just tune out the nasty comments he heard as he rode by —the glances by adults, the long disgusted stares by children. But now, without his pills and mixed with the loss of not playing Santa, he was becoming genuinely unhinged.

Jordan slowly fell into one of his trances. The sporadic people around him turned into blurs but curiously, the occasional insults and snide remarks remained clear as day. Almost as if his subconscious *liked* hearing it. In a way, they made him feel better, stronger. Justifying the brutal actions that he was beginning to fantasize about.

"Jordan, this will be the most memorable Christmas festival this town has ever seen. All because of you. All because of Santa," the voice in his mind whispered. Jordan smiled. He knew what he had to do. Santa would definitely be coming to town this year.

CHAPTER 6: CHERRY FLAVORED SNOW CONE

Jordan rides past his neighbor Steven, who, unsurprisingly, has his friend Craig over once again. Both are the very definition of the ghetto stereotype slobs. Wife-beater tank tops showing off some of the stupidest looking tattoos on Earth. Both men were nursing a few bottles of the cheapest beer you can buy while hanging out in two crappy white lawn chairs on the outside of Steven's equally shitty studio.

"Hey fucker, Christmas ain't for another few days," shouts Steven to Jordan as he wheels up to his porch. Craig laughs and takes a long pull of his beer, shaking his head in agreement to Steven's insult.

Out of his last trance, Jordan glances towards the two men before hopping off his bicycle. Usually, he does his best to avoid his neighbors, especially Steven, who is a giant douchebag. When he's alone he's bad enough. When he's not bumping that awful music he likes, he's shouting "fuck you bitch!" at his opponent in the online shooter game of the week, who is probably a 12-year-old kid. When his friend Craig is around, Steven seems to turn from a *regular* inconsiderate asshole into a *super* inconsiderate asshole.

"Watch this," Steven says to Craig while he places his cheap beer on the ground beside him. Steven lets out a long whistle as he walks over to Jordan, eyeing him up and down. "Damn boy, where the fuck were you? The gay Santa Claus convention?" Both men laugh.

"What do you want, Steven?" asks Jordan, obviously not in the mood for this. " I need to be getting ready," Jordan continues.

"Ready for what, freak? You have a boyfriend coming over to suck your little pecker?" Steven says as he walks back to Craig, laughing. He reaches out with a fist and eagerly receives a fist bump from his friend, who is shaking his head with a wide grin.

"Do you want to see? I can go get part of it real quick and show you, show you both!" Jordan says.

"Sure, dude! Can't wait to see your *My Little Pony* drawings or whatever shit you have in there!"

Jordan quickly unlocks his door and wheels his bike inside. He disappears into the apartment and shuts the door.

"Don't get me wrong, shits funny, man, but you fuck with that guy way too much. He looks like one of those dudes that would snap and shoot up a theater or something," says Craig.

"Nah man, that dudes a little bitch and always has been. I went to school with him. He was a couple of years behind me, but he was the school punching bag. Always doing some weird shit, we just couldn't help ourselves." Steven bends down to pick up the beer he had left behind.

Both men didn't see Jordan reemerge from the studio and didn't notice as he slowly walked behind Steven with a dull vacant look in his eyes.

"Kill them," the voice inside Jordan's head said as he slowly creeped up behind Steven.

"Here, look at this," Jordan said quietly through his trance. He raises a rusty cleaver over his head as Steven turns around to look at him. Steven's smile quickly changes to one of fear as he notices the cleaver. It all happens way too fast for the half-drunken men to react appropriately.

The cleaver comes down brutally across the bridge of Steven's nose, severing it cleanly to the bone. The blade continues downward into his lips, slicing and pulling them off in a gout of blood. The beer seems to fall in slow motion, shattering on the cement followed by some face meat and a steady flow of fresh blood.

Jordan, appearing to live in slow motion through this current trance, has enough time to admire how the fresh blood melted some of the left-over snow from this morning, then mixing with it like a cherry-flavored snow cone.

Steven's hands shoot up to hold his now mangled face, gingerly probing the wound. His eyes bulge in terror as Jordan slowly lifts his head after admiring the bloody snow, his eyes vacant, seeming to peer into his soul.

Steven holds out his hands to defend himself as Jordan starts another series of deadly swings. The first severs three of Stevens's fingers on his right hand; the second blow removes two on his left. Severed fingers join the bloody snow as Jordan delivers the third blow straight into Steven's forehead, getting wedged in the skull. Steven's eyes seem to cross comically before his muscles give up, toppling him to the ground in a heap at Jordan's feet.

Craig never even attempts to flee; he is frozen

by the brutality displayed before him. That was good news for Jordan because he doesn't have to chase him down. Jordan reaches down, placing one foot on Stevens's lifeless chest as he pulls the stuck cleaver free from his forehead. When it pulls free, his head makes a sickening thud as it falls back to the cement.

"Listen, man," Craig starts to say but is cut off by a vicious cleaver swing into the right side of his neck. It takes five swings for the rusty cleaver to sever Craig's head from his body.

When Jordan's trance ends, he finds himself surrounded by blood and the bodies of the two men, and he is happy. For the first time, he feels complete. His trances, once unwelcome embarrassments, now seem to be a blessing. They encourage him, make him stronger.

He surveys the area to make sure nobody saw what he had done. He still has work to do. After all, Santa's work isn't done until Christmas is over. He takes both men and their various severed body parts into his studio, dumping them in the tub. As he goes back outside to clean up the blood, the snow has begun to fall and quickly cover up the scene.

"Well, that takes care of that problem," Jordan says out loud to no one in particular.
Jordan and Steven's apartments are the only ones located in the back corner of the complex, so unless that nosey bitch Susan was out walking her rat of a dog, there was little risk of him being caught.

He enters his studio and pauses at his reflection in the mirror. What looks back at him would be dreadful to everyone. His already disturbing self is now covered in spots of drying blood. He smiles.

CHAPTER 7: PETER

After a long day of setting up the festival, Peter was finishing up when Tony, tailed by Tommy, made his way to him. "How'd auditions go today, guys?" Peter said as they walked up to him, a look of frustration on their faces.

"Shit! Complete and utter shit Peter tha..." Tony holds up his hand, silencing Tommy mid-sentence.

"Not well, Peter. The Santas today, well, you saw them. All of them were garbage, trash, filth! Not a single viable candidate out of today's auditions!" shouted Tony. Peter thought he might go into a tantrum as a spoiled child would.

"Well, that sucks sir, sorry to hear that. It looked like there were a couple of strong candidates walking in," Peter said.

"Your untrained eye wouldn't know a good Santa if it came up and bit you in the ass. Trust me, son, I know these things," said Tony.

"Right." said Peter, holding back his laugher at how fucking ridiculous this man was. *It's a Santa at a church event for God's sake. It's not that fucking hard. Any turd with a pulse could pull it off.* Peter thinks.

"What about him, Tony?" Tommy said, gesturing to Peter, "He's not old enough or big, but shit, Christmas Eve is tomorrow, the event needs a Santa, and we have no others lined up to audition." Tony looked Peter over like he was a fresh piece of cake on display at a diner counter. Both men talked about him as if he wasn't even there.

"Shit," Tommy continued, "We don't even

have to pay the guy. We can just add Santa to his duties." Tony, deep in thought, reluctantly nodded in agreement. A wash of acceptance settled on his face. It was far from perfect, but Tommy was right. They were out of options.

"I'm not going to pretend to like it, but I'm fucking done auditioning for this. I've wasted too much time already. Peter, you're our Santa tomorrow night. Go into the storage room and get what you need for your costume, and for the love of God, at least stuff a pillow into your shirt to give yourself a puffy stomach," said Tony. Both men turn and head back to the office area, leaving Peter to stand in disbelief.

"What the fuck?" Peter said out loud to himself. "Damnit, what am I getting myself into?"

CHAPTER 8:
GOOD CHAT

Jordan is home, hard at work scrubbing his bloodied Santa costume in the kitchen sink. A pile of dirty dishes is quickly filling up with reddish soapy water. Christmas songs gently float through the air from a cheap radio set on the counter. Humming along with "Jingle Bells," Jordan continues his dreadful work.

It has been a few hours since he killed Steven and Craig, and he feels great. The only worry he currently has is the blood-stained Santa suit.

Before settling in for the job, he had taken the time to prop Steven and Craig's bodies at his table. Having dressed them with various leftover Christmas decor streamers, spare lights, some fake snow. The centerpiece being Craig's severed head propped in a big bowl in the center of the table. An old snowman top hat rested on the head while a corncob tobacco pipe jutted out of the lips.

Satisfied with his work, Jordan spreads the costume out on his counter to dry. He is dressed only in his soiled and ill-fitting tighty whities. He notices the medicine bottle and seems to ponder its existence. He grabs it and proceeds to dump its contents down the drain, tossing the now-empty bottle into the room where it bounces off Craig's top hat before landing on the ground in a pool of drying blood.

"You don't need that anymore," says the voice in his head. *"But what you do need to do is get ready. Santa always has his sack of goodies, and you'll need yours too."*

Jordan nods to the voice and walks over to his

bed. There he pulls a dirty, oversized, white pillow-case off a ratty pillow and proceeds to place various items in it. The three bears Peter had given him, his cleaver, and a Phillips head screwdriver. He then walks to his kitchen and searches his dirty dishes for a kitchen knife, which he promptly tosses into his sack.

"What about that?" says the voice.

Jordan goes to the closet and opens it. Among the mismatched shoes and moth-eaten coats is a classic red woodcutting ax. He had purchased it at a rummage sale. As he picks it up, he remembers how the sunlight had glinted off the ax head, catching his eye. Sure he had never used it, never needed to until now. *This will help.* He thinks.

Satisfied with his sack of goodies, he goes and places it by his rusty bicycle.

"What the fuck are you doing, freak!" A voice suddenly sounds behind him, causing him to nearly jump out of his skin.

Jordan whirls around to see Craig's severed head, looking straight at him. "I said, what the fuck are you doing, you sick fuck?" Craig says, spitting out the pipe in the process.

Jordan's look of terror fades and is replaced by one of amusement. *This is new;* he thinks to himself as he walks over and sits in the only vacant seat at the table. "You're, uh, alive?" Asks Jordan.

"No I'm not alive you dumb bastard, my head is obviously not attached to my body. God, you're stupid. And put some fucking pants on," says Craig.

"Nobody wants to see your lil smokey pitching a tent. Gross."

"And put a shirt on too for fuck's sake. You look like a malnourished scarecrow on meth," says Steven. Now apparently also speaking from the dead. His words come out ragged and slurred due to his destroyed mouth. Air hisses out of his empty nose socket with each word, followed by the occasional spurt of dried and crusty blood.

Craig's head laughs at the joke. "Good one, Steven!" Instead of getting mad, Jordan just laughs along with the two of them. Their laughter joins together as "Santa Baby" begins on the radio.

"So who's next Jordan? Did the mailman damage a package of yours and now you need some revenge?" asks Steven

"Or did the pizza guy forget your ranch and now you need to cut off his dick or something?" quips Craig.

"No, I was thinking of starting with that brown nose Tommy and just working my way up from there."

Jordan chuckles as he thinks of how crazy this must look. But hey, this is the longest conversation he's had in a while, not including the audition earlier. Thinking back on that centers him and strengthens his resolve.

"Well fellas, good chat, but I have to get going, don't go anywhere," says Jordan. All three erupt into laughter at the joke. *They're dead; where would they go?* Jordan thinks as he gets ready to leave.

CHAPTER 9: NOT MY FUCKING PROBLEM

Tommy and Tony exit the main hall and into the festival grounds. The decorations are looking great. The food stands are all proudly displayed with gleaming plastic menus. Frozen bananas, hot dogs, funnel cakes, typical fair food. The game stands are all ready to steal unsuspecting people's money as they try to knock down the rigged milk jugs or shoot a basketball through a bent rim. The toy train is busy making a test loop over the stream—good times, and better yet, tax-free money.

Tony checks his watch impatiently as Tommy finishes locking up. "Let me take that for you, Tony," Tommy says as he holds out his hand to receive his boss's heavy side bag.

The men step away from the entrance and into the nearly finished festival. Christmas lights of all colors illuminate their path as they walk through the grounds to their vehicles.

———————

Jordan, complete in his recently cleaned Santa suit, kneels down in some bushes adjacent to the church parking lot. His breath steams out into the chilly winter air. He hasn't decided where he'll kill Tommy, but this is as good a place as any to start. He stalks them through the bushes as they make their way into the main parking area, kitchen knife clutched in his gloved hand. He had hidden his bike along with his Santa sack in the treeline.

————

Having finished for the day, Peter makes his way from a shed near the stream to the front door. "Fuck!" he shouts to himself when he tests the doors to find them locked. He turns and sees Tony and Tommy near their vehicles and takes off at a run to get to them before they leave.

"Take them both now," says the voice in Jordan's head. A look of determination falls over his face. Right before he makes his move out of the bushes towards the men, he pauses as someone shouts.

"Tommy, Tony, hold up a second!" Peter shouts as he jogs up to the two men. "Sorry, but can one of you let me back in? I left my keys and bag in the office."

Jordan watches and waits; the rage inside him threatens to boil over.

"All you, Tommy," says Tony as he takes back his bag from him. "I'm done for the night." Tony says as he walks to his vehicle, a late model black BMW that he had purchased new a few years ago after another successful Christmas celebration.

Tommy lets out an over-the-top sigh and walks over to a nearby truck. A white pickup with rust and bare tires. Clearly, Tommy doesn't get taken care of as much as Tony does by the church profits.

"Let me throw my stuff in the truck, hold on," Tommy says as he unlocks the door and throws in his bag. He slams the door and walks back towards the church, grumbling the whole way.

Jordan waits for Tony to leave before he emerges from the woods, checking his surroundings for any stragglers he may have missed, and makes his way to the truck. He peers inside and tests the handle, pleased that the dumbass left it unlocked. *Big mistake*, he thinks to himself. *This is going to cost you.*

He searches the driver's side compartment before he finds the truck bed shell latch. He pulls it with a satisfying *"clink,"* releasing the catch on the truck bed cover. He lightly shuts the driver's side door and makes his way to the bed of the truck, where he squeezes his way in and pulls the bed cover down, securing it in place.

As he waits for Tommy to return, the voice in his head says, *"Sleepover at Tommy's place!"* A dark grin spreads across Jordan's face exposing his brown teeth as a line of discolored drool streams down his chin.

––––––––––

The two men exit the building; Peter now has his backpack slung over one shoulder as Tommy relocks the doors.

"Remember, no bullshit, just results," Tommy says as he walks back to his truck. Not knowing there is a creepy murderous Santa Claus in the bed. Peter watches him drive off, then slowly strolls through the festival grounds to his car.

Something catches his eye. A gleam from the woodline flashes as Tommy's headlights briefly illuminate it. He walks over to the spot and discovers a bike with a dirty pillowcase propped up next to it. *Isn't this that fucking creepy Santa's bike?* He thinks as he nudges the sack with the toe of his work boot.

"Not my fucking problem," he says out loud as he shrugs his shoulders and walks back to his car.

CHAPTER 10: FUCK YOU, TOMMY

Tommy's drive home was highlighted by Creed's "With Arms Wide Open," blaring from his cheap speakers at full volume. A perfect song for the massive tool that he was. He pulls into the driveway of his small two-bedroom home just as the snow starts to really come down.

Nowhere close to blizzard status, but this would surely add an inch or two to the current amount on the ground.

Jordan, lying down in the bed of the truck with his ear pressed against the tailgate, listens as Tommy parks the truck and shuts it off with a sigh of relief, then proceeds towards his house. Jordan continues to listen to the fading crunch of Tommy's footsteps. He doesn't decide to get out until a few minutes after he hears the front door closing.

Jordan cracks the cover slowly, peering out from the truck bed at his surroundings. In front of him, a castle compared to what he has. Tasteful red brick, black shutters. Then the crown jewel, an ample Christmas display. Red, green, and blue lights hang from the roof edge, as well as those cheap-looking icicle ones. Some inflatable reindeer lightly sway in the winter air as snow steadily piles around them.

He squeezes out of the truck, careful not to make a sound as he surveys the neighborhood. He can't make out anyone in the fading sunlight. It would be that perfect winter dark accentuated by the glow of the lights in a few minutes.

"You should have seen this one guy today, babe, F. R. E. A. K. Freak.

Dude was like 7 feet tall, and rail-thin," Tommy tells his wife Cindy as he sits down at the kitchen table, waiting for the meal that she knows to have ready for him. Cindy, a modest, friendly-looking woman, stands at the kitchen counter, placing under-seasoned but steaming hot food onto two waiting plates. She doesn't know what she saw in Tommy, at least not anymore. But Cindy feels it is too late to start over. So she is content.

"I wish you wouldn't be so mean to people Thomas; you never know what issues in life people are having." Says Cindy.

"Oh, here we go, little miss snowflake at it again," Tommy responds, rolling his eyes as he gets up.

"And here we go, Mr. Badass, because his man-crush Ted Frederick lets him carry his book bags after school today," said Cindy with a smile.

"It's Mr. Frank! Mr. Tony Frank!" Tommy snaps, he grabs his shoes in a huff and exits the kitchen, making his way to the laundry room.

Outside the house, Jordan is thinking of the

best way to get in and make Tommy pay. A light turns on, showing the interior of a laundry room. Tommy shuffles in, shoulders slumped and tosses down a pair of shoes. He looks like someone just pissed in his cheerios. *Little asshole.*

Big windows make it easy for Jordan to follow Tommy's path as he walks from the laundry room to a small office. Sports memorabilia plaster the walls. This must be his literal *little* man cave.

Tommy opens his laptop and sits down for a quick session on *Pornhub*. Cindy calls out that his dinner's getting cold. "In a minute," Tommy responds in an annoyed voice as he unzips his pants.

A wet thud strikes the window beside him, making him jump in his seat. A snowball is slowly sliding down the window, leaving a wet streak. Three more snowballs strike the window in quick succession.

He gets up from his chair and peers out the window while holding up his pants with one hand. The mix of falling snow and darkness makes it impossible for him to see the snowball throwing punk.

"Fucking asshole kids," Tommy says as he grabs a mini commemorative baseball bat off the shelf and heads out of his office towards the front door. Ready to chase off some kids. Hell, maybe he'll even push one over if he gets the opportunity. He's not a manly man, but he feels powerful when talking down to women and children, anybody weaker than him.

Cindy sees him walk by with the bat. "You

know, Thomas, if you just didn't react the way you do, the kids wouldn't pick on you."

"They're not picking on me; I'm not a child! I'm a man!" Tommy says defensively, sounding quite a bit like a petulant child.

He flings the door open and quickly walks outside, puffing his chest and slamming the door, cutting off Cindy's retort in the process. An oversized snowball hits him square in the face, temporarily blinding him. He frantically wipes it away and is struck hard in the head. He falls to the ground in a heap, stunned and dazed.

"Ho Ho Ho asshole," Jordan says as he walks up to the stunned Tommy. Jordan rubs his fist with some snowball, easing the pain after punching Tommy in the face.

Tommy recovers from his daze and wipes the remaining snow from his eyes. He blinks, bringing the towering nightmare into focus. Jordan stands over him in his ill-fitting costume. Something shiny sticks out of his waistband.

"You?" Tommy says incredulously. "That freak from the tryouts today. What the fuck are you doing here?"

Jordan throws another snowball into Tommy's face and pulls out the knife. He stalks towards Tommy as the weak little man continues to wipe the snowball remnants from his face. A trickle of blood leaks from his nose where Jordan had punched him.

He looks up just as Jordan brings the knife

down in a powerful arc. The blade lets out a loud *thunk* as it embeds into Tommy's skull which reminds Jordan of a rock hitting cement. He leaves the weapon stuck in Tommy's head and steps back to admire his work.

Oddly enough. Tommy doesn't make a sound. He awkwardly grabs at the handle, but it looks like his fingers don't work like they used to. It must have hit an essential part of the brain.

Blood leaks out of Tommy's eyes. He makes noises that sound like words, but like his fingers, his mouth seems not to be working correctly.

Jordan grabs a strand of Christmas lights from Tommy's display. He notes that removing that strand did not affect the other lights, which he is grateful for. Wouldn't want to ruin the decorations after all. Jordan wraps the lights around Tommy's throat and starts squeezing. "Fuck you, Tommy!" Jordan hisses through clenched teeth as he chokes the life out of him. Tommy's feet kick out uselessly into the snow and eventually fade. With one last choked-off gasp, he stops moving.

He heaves Tommy's twitching body onto his shoulder and dumps him into the passenger side seat of the truck. Jordan searches his pockets for the truck keys but can't find them.

———

Cindy is annoyed that her husband is still messing around outside. Tired of waiting for him while her food gets cold, she takes her meal into the living room to at least watch some TV while she eats. She hears the door open but doesn't bother turning around.

"Dinner's on the table Thomas," she says as she flips through the channels.

Jordan walks behind her, some fresh blood on his costume. He makes a fist as if to strike Cindy. The thrill of killing Tommy moments ago still flows through his veins. He gets within striking distance and stops.

The smell of her cooking makes his mouth water. He does a quick inventory of the room, noticing that there isn't another plate of food for Tommy, which means that it must still be in the kitchen.

He glances around the living room one more time but doesn't see the keys. He walks to the kitchen and finds them next to a plate of fried chicken and mashed potatoes. Before taking the keys, he sits down quietly and calmly eats the food.

What an image this would be for Cindy. Walking in, seeing this bloody Santa eating her food. Blood drips onto the plate, but he doesn't care. He hears Cindy laughing at the television. *This must be what normalcy feels like.* After finishing his meal, he slowly exits the home and gets in the truck. Cindy remains watching her favorite show not knowing that a crazed killer Santa had been inches away from her.

Jordan drives away. His dead passenger is safely seated next to him.

CHAPTER 11: TABLE OF CORPSES

It's 9 PM by the time Jordan makes it home, his co-pilot sitting dead beside him. He had managed to find an old baseball cap in the truck, which he placed on Tommy's head to conceal the embedded knife. He missed his bike and felt naked without his Santa sack, but the truck will be helpful for what he has planned.

He rolls up to his designated parking space and puts the truck in park. "You know, this is the first time I've actually had my own car in my spot." Jordan says.

"Uh, it's not *your* truck asshole," Jordan looks over at Tommy, not at all surprised to see his corpse looking back at him under the brim of the cap. "So technically, this is the first time that *MY* truck has been in your spot. You psycho cocksucker," says Tommy.

"You sound pretty great for having a knife in your brain." Jordan says as he pulls the keys out of the ignition and looks around the parking lot, checking for any possible witnesses.

"Fuckkkk youuuuu. Did you do this because of the Santa tryouts?" Says Tommy with a smile on his face. Jordan looks away, refusing to make eye contact with the corpse. "It is, damn dude, you really are a freak. It's a Santa tryout for a one-night gig. Get the fuck over yourself for God's sake. You swear it's the fucking lead role in Titanic or something." Says Tommy.

Jordan gets out of the truck and makes his way to the passenger side door. A light snow is falling. He can still hear Tommy's muffled voice from inside the truck. Mostly curse words and insults. Even in death, Tommy still has his same winning personality.

Satisfied that the coast is clear, Jordan opens the door and pulls Tommy's body out. It falls face first with a loud crunch in the fresh snow.

"Oh, just great," Tommy mumbles as Jordan shuts the door and begins dragging the dead weight of Tommy into his apartment. Once inside, Jordan props Tommy up in the last available chair at the table of corpses. Tommy's eyes flicker over Steven and Craig's bodies.

"Sup new guy," the severed head of Craig says, welcoming Tommy. "So I bet you're wondering how you ended up here?" Craig and Steven crack up at the apparently inside joke.

———

Jordan carefully strips down into his underwear, meticulously hanging up the Santa costume. He's too tired to spot clean the new bloodstains out; he'll just have to make do with what he has. He gets his phone and sets the alarm for 3 hours. He'll take a power nap before going out to handle Tony.

Jordan, full from his impromptu meal at Tommy's, crawls into his bed, and despite the constant mockery and bickering from the corpses at the table, falls deeply asleep.

Tomorrow is Christmas Eve. He dreams of

reindeer flying, Santa laughing, Christmas cookies, and cheer. For the first time in a long time, Jordan feels whole.

CHAPTER 12: JINGLE BELLS

It wasn't hard finding out where Tony lived. All Jordan had to do was look at Tommy's map's history in his phone, which he was nice enough to bookmark as "bosses crib," which is super fucking lame. Jordan's quick power napped proved to be more than enough of a recharge.

He made a slow drive-by to get the lay of the neighborhood. Tony's car was parked in the front, close to the garage door, which was conveniently left open. The area is upper middle class, with ample space between neighbors and some thick woods behind the houses. He turns off his lights and parks on the curb. He surveys the neighborhood and is pleased to find nobody out.

Perfect, he thinks. *I'll have plenty of time to set up before going in to deal with Tony.*

After he finishes his setup in the woods behind Tony's house, he heads into the open garage. Toys litter the area—a pink bike with those streamers hanging from its handlebars. A black superhero scooter with the paint chipped off from hours of use, and various action figures and dolls in different states of disrepair. These were clearly the outside toys, not meant to be inside.

He puts his ear to the door leading into the house and listens. After a few minutes of nothing, he checks the doorknob and finds that it's unlocked. He slowly opens it and peers into a dark mudroom.

Well, Tony, you should have locked your door, dumbass. He enters, slowly making his way throughout the house. Hearing voices from the second story, he slowly creeps up the stairs, cleaver in one hand, the santa sack over his shoulder. He passes a room that is obviously a child's. A large KEEP OUT sign is scribbled on some red construction paper and taped to the wall. He reaches for the doorknob but stops at the sound of a voice.

He can just make out Tony's voice emanating from up the hall. He decides the kid can wait. He passes another child's room, this one marked by a superhero poster taped on the door, and makes his way to the last door. Blue tinted light peeks out from the crack in the door—a faint voice of a sports announcer filters through the gap towards Jordan.

A door cracks open behind him. A little boy peers out from the crack in his doorway. Sleep distorts his features, and he rubs his eyes to wake up. Once his vision clears, the boy's eyes light up.

"Santa?" he says, a hint of wonder in his voice. "Is that really you? You're skinnier than I thought." Jordan rests his cleaver against the wall beside him and flings his sack off of his shoulder.

He walks over to the boy, digging into the sack as he goes. The boy lights up in anticipation. Santa, here in his own house, looking for a toy to give him. Jordan's fingers tighten around what he needs.

Jordan pulls out a teddy bear, one that Peter had given him before his audition. Jordan fondly looks at the bear before giving it to the boy. His fingers stretch out in anticipation of the gift. He accepts it and gives it a giant hug. Jordan gestures for the boy to return to his room, turns, and walks away.

"Santa?" The boy calls out. Jordan turns his head and looks at the boy. He brings a bloody hand up to his lips, his pointer finger sticking straight out, rests against his fake beard.

Jordan lets out a quiet "Shhhh" to the boy before returning to the last bedroom door. The boy's door shuts with a soft click behind him.

Jordan peeks in through the crack and sees a shape huddled under the blanket. *Time to die, Tony.* He places his sack on the floor by the door and pulls out the kitchen knife. He conceals it in his waistband. He retrieves his cleaver then enters the room.

Jordan creeps over to the sleeping figure and slams his cleaver down into the mass over and over again. Blood spreads across the sheet, a voice, a woman's, briefly screams out in pain but is quickly silenced by Jordan's repeated blows. The head, torso, and legs are all struck with brutal blows.

He pulls back the sheet, Tony's wife lies bleeding from numerous gashes. Her head is split, her left hand is severed. He delivers one more blow for good measure, leaving the clever stuck in her damaged chest. Blood drips from the bed onto the hardwood floor—*drip, drip, drip.*

Tony is in the master bathroom when he hears his wife scream. Quickly he runs to the attached closet and grabs his locked handgun case. Tony fumbles with the lock before finally getting it unsecured. He rams a loaded magazine into the 40 caliber pistol and explodes out of the bathroom.

A tall skinny Santa Claus was standing over

his wife. Her blood and bits of her littering the area. A cleaver sticks in a gaping hole on her chest. He doesn't hesitate. *Boom, boom, boom,* three shots go out in rapid succession.

The first two go wide, striking the wall behind Jordan showering him in bits of paint and drywall. The third hits him in the neck. Jordan's blood sprays the wall behind him; he falls to the ground clutching the wound, then lies still.

Tony backs his way towards his room door, keeping his eyes on Santa's body. "Kids!?" He calls over his shoulder. After a few moments, both doors open. A little boy's face, 8-year-old Jimmy, and a girl, 12-year-old Holly, peer out. Sleep and terror both fighting for position on their faces.

"Holly, take your brother and stay in your room. Do not open the door for anyone." The kids remained frozen. "Do it, you little shits!" Tony yells. The boy runs into his sister's room, still clutching the bear. She slams the door shut behind them. Tony turns his full attention back to Jordan's form.

He inches over, barrel trained on the man who has fallen on his side facing away from Tony. He nudges him with his foot, once then twice. Satisfied that he is dead, he puts his gun in his pocket and kneels over Santa. He rolls him over and stands up with a shock at the realization of who it is.

"No fucking way. This fucking freak!" Tony yells.

In one fluid motion, Jordan grabs the kitchen knife that he had concealed in his waistband and drives it into Tony's bare foot, severing the big toe in the process. Tony screams in pain and falls to the ground. Jordan pulls himself into a crawling position and slithers his way on top of Tony.

The gunshot wound to Jordan just grazed the skin. Lots of blood at first but nothing fatal. Tony puts his hand into his pocket to retrieve his gun, but Jordan is ready. He brings the knife down and stabs it through Tony's pants pocket into his hand, impaling his hand to his thigh. He leaves the blade wedged in there and stands up.

Tony looks up in a state of shock. *How can this happen? I'm Tony fucking Franks. I run this shit.* Tony thinks as Jordan saunters over to him.

"Quick and painless or long and painful?" Jordan asks as he stands to his full height. He reaches over and pulls the cleaver from Tony's dead wife's body.

"Wha..what?" Tony stutters.

"You know what mother fucker! Quick and painless or long and pain.." he cuts off as Tony manages to get to his feet and runs into the bathroom. Jordan exaggeratedly rolls his eyes and lumbers after him, the voice in his head whispering words of encouragement.

Jordan explodes through the door, teeth bared and fists clenched. A door leads to an outside balcony. He goes through it and emerges onto a small wood balcony complete with two small chairs and a table.

Tony lunges at him from behind the door,

hand still impaled into his thigh. Whatever grace he had when he took the shots at Jordan is now gone. He reverts back to his idiot self. His attack, fast but uncoordinated, is easily sidestepped by Jordan, who gives him a shove.

Aided by his momentum Tony falls over the railing down into the snowy yard below. He lands with a loud crunch. His breath explodes from his body as he rolls in pain. He painfully gets to his feet and looks up at Jordan.

"Fuck you mother fucker!" He flips Jordan off and stumbles into the backyard towards the woods, heading towards some lights coming from just inside the treeline. As he gets closer, he hears soft music playing, "Auld Lang Syne" floats softly through the air. Tony doesn't think how random and out of place this is. He pushes through the first few branches and enters into a clearing of horrors.

Bodies, blood, and appendages litter the area. The corpse of a man, hideously beaten and bloody, is tied around a tree by a wrapping of lit Christmas lights. A cell phone pokes out of the corpse's front pocket, the source of the song. He takes a few steps closer towards the corpse, its features coming into view. Tommy stares back at him with lifeless eyes. He hears a voice from his left.

"Jingle bells…." Jordan's voice sings out with a demented tone.

Tony looks towards the source of the sound but only sees a headless corpse propped sitting against an old stump, it's head complete with top hat resting in the lap.

"Jingle bells..." Jordan's voice sounds out, now behind Tony. He whirls around but once again is not met by Jordan, but by another corpse, this one with the face mangled, its nose missing.

"Jingle all, the way," Jordan steps into the clearing, his cleaver in his hand caked in gore from Tony's wife. "Time's up, asshole." Jordan says through a grin.

Tony falls to his knees, tears stream down his face, snot bubbles from his nostrils. "Please, listen, I'm sorry." Tony pleads as Jordan steps closer to him, cocking his head as the voice inside him whispers. Jordan nods and steps closer.

"Jack, right? Just please listen" Tony attempts to pull the knife free of his impaled hand, but his fingers are numb from the snow, and he is getting weak from blood loss.

"Cute kids," Jordan says as he kneels, getting face to face with Tony. "Don't worry; I'm not a total prick like you. Judging how you treated me, a complete stranger, I can only guess how you treat them. They'll be better off without you."

Tony's face switches from panic to shock as Jordan drives the cleaver into his stomach. Tony falls backward and lays on the ground.

Blood seeps from his new wound, bubbling around the cleaver and soaks the snow. Jordan stands and watches as Tony's life fades away. He carefully places his shoe on Tony's throat and presses down. Tony's eyes bulge as he gasps from the lack of oxygen. Jordan watches as life fades from Tony's eyes.

Without fanfare, he takes his time walking back through the woods and into the backyard. He passes by the balcony where Tony had fallen from. The imprint his body made in the snow is slowly being refilled by the falling snow.

He makes his way to the front of the house. The two children stand in the doorway; the boy clutches the bear to his chest. The little girl holds Jordan Santa's sack. He walks up to her and takes it. Jordan reaches in and pulls out another bear, handing it to her and ruffling both of their hair.

"Merry Christmas. Probably should just go to the neighbor's house. There's nothing left in there for you." He turns and walks back toward Tommy's truck, his job far from over.

CHAPTER 13:
THE FESTIVAL

While security guards are busy directing people into safe parking spots, taking extra caution in the snowy conditions, Peter suits up in the employee bathroom. Tony and Tommy, surprising everyone, have yet to show.

"What the fuck am I doing?" Peter says, looking at himself in the mirror, freshly dressed head to toe in the church's Santa costume. "Watch out, ladies, Santa's *coming* tonight," he laughs at his own joke and exits the bathroom.

———————————

Jordan takes extra time getting ready for tonight. It is Christmas Eve after all, and the night of the big festival! The night this town would remember forever. He is driving Tommy's truck as casually as possible, considering he's a 6 foot 3 inch Santa Claus.

He manages to be waved through by security, taking a mental note of the two security guards whispering and laughing as he drives by. *They must be talking about him. I'll make them pay too.*

The time is now 6 PM, and the festival is in full swing. The parking lot hasn't had a new car arrive in a while, so the security guards begin making their rounds. Usually, things are quiet, but you never know if someone might try to take advantage of the event and break into some vehicles.

Having taken his seat on the Santa throne flanked by two teenage elves, Peter begins seeing kids for their yearly gift begging sessions followed by a quick picture or two, for $19.99 of course. *I don't understand how old dudes could do this job every year. Some of the kids smell like straight poop.* Peter thinks as he does his best at being jolly and merry. It's only for one night after all.

Jordan sits in the truck and checks his reflection one last time in the rearview mirror. He picked a spot closest to the woodline to recover his other Santa sack. Hopefully, it wasn't touched during the night; if so, he'll have to improvise. A tap on the driver's side door pulls him from his thoughts, followed by a bright flashlight shining into his face.

"Hey man, I sincerely hope you're not beating the meat in there?" a Security Guard says.

A young man no older than 19 stares in at Jordan, a fragile air of authority flows out of him. Jordan steps out of the truck and brings himself to his full height, towering over the young guard.

Jordan grabs the man by the throat in a death grip. Surprisingly organized for just having been seized by this Santa monstrosity, the guard pulls a baton from his belt and jabs it into Jordan's side. Jordan lets out a rush of air in response to the hit, blowing his rancid smelling breath into the guard's face causing him to gag.

Jordan hears footsteps and turns in time to see another security guard, an older man clearly trying to enjoy the waning years of his life, swinging his baton down towards Jordan's back. The strike bounces off Jordan with a dull thud.

"Let go of him you son of a bitch!" the old guard shouts as he readies another strike.

The man is just a bit too slow with delivering his strike, Jordan lashes out and grabs the baton in mid-swing and twists it violently out of the guard's hand.

He gives a final squeeze to the young guard's throat and violently pushes him down into the snow. He turns his attention to the old guard. Jordan swings the baton in a backhanded motion against his face. Teeth and blood briefly reflect in the light before disappearing into the night.

Jordan laughs joyfully at the gruesome sight of the flying blood and teeth.. The old guard stumbles on his feet before being struck again over the top of the head, splitting his scalp in a sickening crack. He falls to his knees in a daze. Jordan admires his bloody baton and slowly walks up to the kneeling man. He bends over and wipes the blood off on the guard's shirt.

Jordan kicks him in the center of his chest, causing him to fling back into the ground, knocking the air out of him in the process. "Leave him alone you fucker," rasps the young guard.

The young guard gets up on shaky legs and charges Jordan, attempting to tackle him to the ground. Jordan's skinny, but he manages to absorb the attempted tackle and pushes him off. Jordan brings the baton in a wide arc down, connecting with a sickening CRACK against the young man's temple.

Jordan grabs him by the hair and hits him over and over again with the baton. Blood, teeth, and bits of hair all splat across the pavement.

He lets the young man fall to the ground, stands over him, and brings his Converse shoe down violently into his face. He repeatedly stomps until the boy's features are barely recognizable. Blood, brain, and bits of bone cake over Jordan's shoe.

"Great." he says, as he shakes his leg in an attempt to shake loose some of the gore. He manages to shake free a few pieces of matter before giving up.

Jordan breathes heavily, but he's not done yet. He looks for the older man but can't find him. He does see a trail of blood and disturbed snow. He follows, surprised about how far he managed to get into the woods in his current state.

"End of the line old man," Jordan stands over the old guard and rolls him onto his side. He lashes out, but he's so weak that the punch doesn't even make it to Jordan's face.

"Can't say you didn't try buddy, now open your fucking mouth." The man, frightened out of his mind, refuses, feebly shaking his head back and forth. Eyes wide, he stairs up into Jordan's face.

Jordan shouts his command again, "I said open your fucking mouth, cocksucker!"

The old guard reluctantly agrees and slowly opens it, sniffling in shame and fear. Jordan slams the baton into his open mouth and leans on to it with his chest, wedging the baton down as far as it can go, scraping against the man's teeth similar to the sound of nails against a chalkboard. With his hands now free, Jordan pinches shut the man's nose and holds his head steady as the old guard struggles to breathe.

It takes him a few minutes to die. Jordan almost grows bored as he suffocates the man, letting out a huge yawn during the middle of the savage act.

Having finished off the two guards, he gathers his ax from his sack and makes his way towards the festival.

———

Harold Jones left the funnel cake counter to fetch some more powdered sugar from the stack of supplies nearby. He didn't notice the dark figure standing in the shadows at first. He squints and the image before him makes him shudder involuntarily.

A tall man in a Santa outfit smiles at him behind a bloody fake white beard. An ax cradled in Santa's hands. Without warning, Santa sprints at Harold, bringing the ax around in a wide arc. Harold doesn't even have time to put up his hands in a feeble defense as the ax head strikes him in the left shoulder. Then the stomach. He falls to his knees.

Harold looks up in a state of shock as the killer

flips the ax around, so the flat side faces him. He raises it above his head as if he were getting ready to hit the bell on those carnival games with the giant oversized mallet. The ax blade comes down and ends Harold's life. Jordan laughs as he repeatedly brings the flat part of the ax down into the man's head, causing it to burst like an overripe watermelon.

He takes a second to admire his kill, then moves on to the next stand. People, enthralled with stuffing their faces with greasy food or playing games, overlook the horror walking just out of the reach of the Christmas lights.

———

Steve Whitaker loved his BBQ set. The redwood handled spatula, the extra-long tongs, even the gleaming metal skewers he was currently using to roll the hot dogs. He lived for grilling. His *"I'd rather be grilling"* apron proudly draped over his chest.

"Hot dog or burger?" Steve asks a young couple who have stepped up to his grilling stand.

They go to answer when suddenly blood erupts across both of their faces. Steve's left eye protrudes out, the gristle and tendons stretch out of his head, almost looking like a wet guitar string. One of his prized skewers punctures out of the retina; white goop drips off of it and onto the hot grill, sizzling and smoking along with the various meats.

Steve falls face-first into his red hot grill. Ash from the impacted charcoal explodes into the air in a cloud of redness.

The young couple screams at Jordan, his blood-splattered face illuminated behind the smoke. He has another skewer in his free hand with a steaming hotdog attached; he takes a bite and winks at the couple. The bloody ax was held loosely in his other hand. The couple runs, screaming through the middle of the festival.

The entire festival seems to freeze in place and slowly turn their heads toward where the couple is pointing. Steven, the BBQ guy, has now caught on fire. His skin is starting to sizzle along with the BBQ meat, but they don't focus on that.

They focus on the disgusting Santa that limps from behind the grill and fully into the light. Jordan's eyes flutter as he raises his head towards the sky; a light snow shower has started. The flakes fall and become stuck in the fresh blood on his face. Chaos erupts as everyone has the same idea- run. It makes it easier for Jordan.

Santa severs Cole Dyer's head clean from his shoulders as he attempts to run past him, the blood fountains into the air, severed head landing with a plop into a nearby cotton candy machine, thumping along while getting wrapped up in the sugary goodness.

Suzie Carter, temporarily wheelchair-bound after last month's soccer injury, attempts to roll away after being abandoned by her group of friends.

Her injured left leg is locked into the footrest and extended straight out. Jordan, without a word, walks over and stomps his foot down into her straight knee. The leg snaps backward, the damaged foot now sticking into the air at an unnatural angle. She screams, he laughs.

Peter has a little girl on his lap, listening to her wants and desires when the chaos happens. Initially, he thinks it was just kids playing a prank. But then he sees the blood.

"Shit, is that Jordan from the other day dressed, dressed as fucking Santa?" he mutters to himself. He feels like he is in a twisted dream.

"Why the fuck is Santa such a big deal in this fucking town?!" He flings the girl off his lap and into the snow. "Sorry!" he yells to her parents as he shoulders his way through them and towards the violence, a look of determination etched into his face.

He runs around a corner and slides to a stop in the snow. Jordan is holding a middle-aged woman by her ponytail, a bloody ax in his other hand. He drags her over to a nearby table, grabbing a steak knife along the way. He runs it across her throat. A thin line of skin separates before erupting into a waterfall of blood as he flings her into the seating area, collapsing a folding table in the process.

Despite the savageness in front of him, Peter notices the blank expression on Jordan's face, the emptiness in his eyes.

Jordan looks at Peter and finally seems to see him, actually see who is standing there.

"You? They gave you the fucking role?" Jordan drops the ax to his side. He cannot believe it. *What does Peter have that he doesn't?* "Did you even want to be Santa?"

"Listen, man. You can stop this right now; nobody else has to get hurt." Says Peter.

"DID YOU EVEN WANT IT!?" Jordan shouts at Peter, picking up the ax and gripping it tightly. Spit flying from his mouth.

"Dude, you're fucking crazy, it is just a church Santa, chill out," replies Peter.

"It's not *JUST* a church *SANTA*! It's my dream, my life. And you fucking took it from me!" Jordan walks towards him during this outburst. Peter steps back, careful not to trip over anything. Falling right now would be a death sentence with this killer Santa stalking him with an ax.

They are heading out of the main festival area towards the stream. Unfortunately for Peter, the ice isn't thick enough, so it's too dangerous to try to get across. He'd more than likely fall through and then get swept up in the current and freeze to death before he could manage to pull himself out. He'll have to run, or he'll have to fight.

"Dude, I didn't do shit to you. I gave you those fucking bears for God's sake," Peter stops as he reaches the bank of the stream. Jordan seems to consider this. *Damn, he really did give me those sweet stuffed bears*. Jordan thinks.

Police sirens begin to sound in the distance and are closing in fast. The voice, fearing that Jordan is having a change of heart, whispers out to him. *"He took it, that was yours, and he took it from you."* Jordan lets out a cry of rage and sprints at Peter, swinging wildly with his ax.

Peter just managed to side-step out of the deadly ax path and punches Jordan as hard as he can in the face, dazing him in the process.

Peter strikes him again, the gross Santa beard rips off of Jordan's face and flies off into the stream and is quickly swept downstream. Jordan brings the handle of the ax up and drives it into Peter's nose, breaking it on impact. Peter falls on his back, clutching his bleeding nose.

Jordan slowly walks over to Peter and stands over him. Jordan brings the ax up over his head, ready to deliver the final death blow. Peter kicks out, connecting with Jordan's balls with a sickening crunch.

Pain instantly washes over Jordan, his eyes roll back in his head as he drops the ax, which sticks in the snow inches away from Peters's head. Spit and blood explode out of Jordan's mouth with a rush of air, spraying across Peters's damaged face.

Peter scrambles to his feet, pulling the ax out of the snow; he puts it on his shoulder like a baseball bat. Jordan, still clutching his crotch, howls in pain. He lets out a shriek as Peter brings the ax around, flat edge out, into the side of his knee cap with a loud crack. Jordan collapses to one knee; his head bowed in pain.

Peter goes to hit him again but hesitates.

"You're...not...Santa," Jordan squeezes the words out between his rotten teeth.

"Yeah, well, neither are you fucker," Peter raises the ax over his head, flipping it so the blade is facing down.

"Merry Christmas, bitch." Peter says.

He brings the ax down in a powerful arc into the back of Jordan's head, blood sprays from Jordan into Johnny's open mouth. When the edge connected, the sound it made reminded Peter of a home run ball he hit a few years ago at a softball game. The blood splattering into his face took him out of the brief trance.

Jordan, with a final whimper, falls forward and tumbles into the stream, the ax head, still partially embedded into Jordans skull, lets out a long sucking *squelch* sound as it pulls from his head. Peter follows Jordan's body as it travels under the model train bridge before disappearing around a bend.

"Drop it asshole!" a loud commanding voice shouts from behind Peter.

Peter, still in a frenzy of rage, spins rapidly towards the threatening voice. A few feet away stands a police officer with a shotgun pointed at him. Peter's brain doesn't work, and he can't form the words to tell the cop that everything is ok, that the real killer, Jordan, is dead. That he just brained him with a fucking ax, that his body fell into the stream. He takes a step towards the officer.

A 3-inch slug punches into Peter's chest,

erupting out his back. Blood and bits of bone spray the snow. He hears the shotgun blast a second later. The shot causes him to stumble back to the edge of the stream, teetering on the edge of the bank. The officer, ready to end this killer Santa rampage, racks the shotgun, takes careful aim, and blows Peter's head apart, spraying the snow with his blood, brains, and bits of the Santa hat fabric.

The smell of gunpowder mixes with the sweet smells of fried treats and tasty festival foods. Screams and sirens compete with the cheerful Christmas music floating through the church grounds.

The snow continues to fall as Jordan's body, still clad in his cherished Santa costume, floats down the stream in blood filled water.

The End

ABOUT THE AUTHOR

Todd Condit

Lover of all things horror. Reader of books, watcher of movies. Father, husband, and all around BBQ lover.

Printed in Great Britain
by Amazon

87198973R00050